I0520076

Sissy & Juju

…...a sibling story

Dedicated to the "f" Troop and cuzins

Create Inspire Grow
Publishing

Brooke Dale

Sissy and JuJu

Light shines in from the smallest hole, and from that hole he could see flashes, back and forth, resembling shadows. His eyes could do nothing but fill with tears. Sadness overcame his body, and so did weakness and feelings of dismay.

"BOOM" against the closet door, where he was hiding.'crash,boom,bang,boom,crash,bang, the sounds of glass breaking, doors slamming and reopening again, furniture smashing and only his imagination could wonder what else.

Julian heard for hours the screaming, the crying, the breaking of glass. It was like a never ending groundhogs day, just like the movie, being stuck in the same day over and over. If only he had the courage to open the closet door.

Julian was 10 years old when his mother left him and sister Sissy, short for Cecilia, she was 14. Their mother never said goodbye, and that began writing their sibling story.

She never kissed them on their foreheads or pulled them to her chest to hug or comfort them before leaving. She never reassured them of her return or that in her absence everything would be all right.

She never said, "I'll be back". She never said she was leaving, their mother just left. Cecelia and Julian woke up and she was gone.

Sissy was in the kitchen making "good ole hot cereal", and had the oven open for the extra heat. When he entered the kitchen, he entered with a blanket draped around himself like a ghost.

He sat in the chair across from the stove and asked, "Where's mama, Sissy?"

"Eat ya food, JuJu, it's gon' get cold."

"But where's ?"

"'Eat ya food, JuJu, we ain't got no mama no mo', no daddy, we ain't got nobody but us, now eat!"

Sissy slammed the spoon down on the counter, dropped her head for a few moments, and just walked away with sounds of whimpers following her.

Being 14 years old and an instant mother weighed instantly on her spirit. She felt like she was going to break, but she knew that she couldn't. She was actually already broken, but exactly how she was broken would soon be revealed.

JuJu couldn't eat, he just swirled his spoon around and around in the bowl as he went inside his own mind. Juju had a hard time mentally as well.

They were struggling, lying to school teachers and anyone who asked about their mother or situation. They were extremely creative with their stories so they did manage with minimal help over time. The neighbors knew they were good children and honestly had their own problems so they never confirmed the mother was gone.

These two children literally had no one. but an aunt and uncle that were nowhere to be found. The sad reality was not many people cared if the mother was present or not. Sissy and Julian didn't have any family and because of their mothers relationships with men, they had no family friends either. Their mothers siblings had passed, an older brother from drugs and the sister from heart failure. Sissy and JuJu were all alone.

4

JuJu was always in that moment in his mind where he was back in that closet everyday and every night hearing the screams and the cries, the banging breaking of glass. At the end of that night showed blood on the walls, telling a story JuJu wasn't ready to hear.

His eyes had seen more than he had bargained for. JuJu was scarred with the pain, bruised with turmoil and abandonment, something many know a lot about, admittedly or not.

School Terror and Holiday Blues

"JuJu. Juju.........JUJU.. Sissy repeatedly yelled, startling JuJu as he dropped his bowl, flipping it upside down.. always with the good ole cereal

When their mother left, the school year was just beginning. The siblings tried to maintain as long as they could. When the holidays rolled around, what seemed like small things were now much more noticeable. No gifts, no new clothes, no tree or decorations for Christmas or New Years Eve.

"Dang Sissy whatcha' do that foe?" JuJu replied.

"Boy, I been calling you, ... come on get cleanup so you can get to school."   Sissy said to JuJu, while trying to push him along.

I ain't going to school no mo', ain't nobody bout to laugh at me today no mo' days, Sissy I mean it , no mo'', shaking and hanging his head low.

Somehow, they managed through the year, both birthdays and even the deadliest of winter and even the summer heat. JuJu, however, could not see himself enduring the ridicule or mental anguish again.

The teasing, bullying, he just could not see himself taking on that again another year. JuJu ran out to what now has become his safety space, the closet. He refused to come out. He wept through the door and Sissy just sat on the other side on the floor, touching the door, weeping herself. She felt her brother's pain but what could she do?

Sissy sat by that door, for hours at a time, day in and day out. It had become their 'new norm'. She slid her fingers under the door, wiggled them around, hoping to feel JuJu's hand.Finally, his fingers grabbed hers. "Nobody will ever hurt you JuJu...ever", said Sissy.

"Sissy, Sissy " ......JuJu ran top speed in the house. "Sissy, Sissy, it's mama, I saw her, I saw her we gotta go back, we gotta go back and get her..."

Sissy ran from her room asking JuJu what was all the yelling about. He was so out of breath, bent over holding his knees....

"I saw her, by the store, she was outside the store,...this guy.. and, and...I yelled her name but..I don't know if she heard me. So I just ran home to get you Sissy before she left...Come on!, before she goes.."

JuJu pulled at Sissy continuously but she was unresponsive. "Stop JuJu, just STOP! She's not gon' be there, she's NOT OUR MAMA! JuJu, we ain't got no mama. She don't care about you or me, she left us, with nothing, and you betta believe she heard you and she didn't care. I'm our mama now. She left us at 10 and 14 years old JuJu We kids! Is that a mama, huh?"

"'Stop it Sissy, jus' come on, please, before she goes. ", cried JuJu, Sissy did not budge.

"I'm going" JuJu yelled, as he ran out the door as fast as he could.

The reality of his mother's abandonment would dwell in his tortured memories and he willingly visited that dark place too often.

To no one's surprise, when JuJu returned, their mother was gone. In fact, the entire crowd had disbursed, the corner was empty and JuJu wondered if it was all in his mind and began to wonder was he in fact imagining the entire thing? Seeing his mother beaten whipped, abused and then being *abandon*ed had severely traumatized him.

JuJu walked home in a slump with his head hung low, he didn't know what to feel. Sissy told him not to go.

All he knew was that he had lost his mother, yet again, and he was tired of watching his sister struggle as a teenager to take care of them.

His heart was heavy for her, every time Sissy left the house to do odd jobs, before, in between and after school. JuJu was at a CROSSROAD...

He continued to struggle with depression, although he didn't know what he was feeling. He saw images flashing through his thoughts all day of a man the streets called, Red, a.k.a. Billy.

JuJu hadn't seen Billy since the day his mother left but he could never forget that face. Oddly, the hidden mystery was that JuJu secretly admired Billy for the command he had over women nor did he truly hate him.

The Writings on the Walls

Do you know you can hate someone and admire them? It may not be their character you like but you can somehow respect them. Is that crazy? Not ambivalence , but possible admiration? Maybe? What was or is to be admired or desired? Especially about someone you hate or despise.

JuJu was growing but he was also growing more confused, and his mind was not maturing naturally. He began sketching and drawing images in the closet where he would lock himself, safety zone.

Even though it was only-him and Sissy, he would still go into the closet but, now with the door cracked for hours, and he would sit and draw on the walls. The writing was truly becoming clear on those walls for JuJu, Sissy tried but deep down she knew she couldn't control her brother.

They argued and he became more and more defiant.

She was trying to raise a boy who was growing into a young man and all while trying to teach herself how to become a woman all while only being a young girl herself.

His respect for women lessened by the day as he saw them degrading themselves around him more and more, with men and drugs prostitution on television and in his neighborhood, it was everywhere around JuJu. The only positive female influence in JuJu's life was Sissy and he did not need that to change.

One afternoon Sissy was cleaning and the closet door was cracked. She never went into that closet, but why would she? This day, however, there was a strange feeling overcoming her entire body as she passed by. She opened the door and what she saw made her cringe from head to toe.

Sissy became light-headed, her vision blurry, her forehead covered with sweat, as she stared at the closet painted with red.

Is this...? Could this be..? Is this Blood..?

She began to sweat profusely and feeling nauseated and weak at the knees, as she caught herself against the wall, her hand felt moist. Her head began to pound and she began to stumble. She fell back and slid down the wall. At that moment she began to reflect on JuJu. It was like her life began to flash and she started to black out. Moments and images of his hand being cut and excuses that he'd made.

What was he doing to himself? This image he was trying to draw, it was so scrambled and so destructive, so distorted, but yet still so clear because it looked like... no it couldn't be...

Sissy cried and tears filled her hands and when she went to wipe her own face,.... blood, OH MY GOD! she yelled, jumping up, and running from the closet. At that moment remembering the fact that the walls were covered with blood ,his blood... but yet when she looked at her hands again, there was nothing there but tears.

Was this her imagination? Was her mind playing tricks on her?

She slammed the closet door. She had seen what she had seen, and she had indeed felt what she felt. Sissy called and called out for JuJu, but he didn't answer. She sat at the kitchen table for hours, alone and confused, her mind completely tormented about what had happened.

JuJu had been gone all day and Sissy hadn't moved from that spot at the table once she had sat there. Suddenly, a knock at the door and when she opened it to her surprise and not a good one, it was none other than....Red a.k.a Billy!

JuJu Returns

JuJu had been gone now for what seemed like months, but had actually been a few days. Where he had been, what he'd seen and what he'd been doing was unknown. Yet after he returned, nothing was the same anymore.

JuJu returned with a new pair of shoes, a new jacket and carrying a medium sized bag. Inside the bag would contain an item that could possibly change who JuJu would become forever. When he saw Sissy again, he could tell there was something different about her. She seemed tired, less aggressive, and noticeably different. She wasn't so motherly anymore. She wasn't questioning him or as concerned as she usually was or should have been, as far as he was concerned.

"What's wrong Sissy", asked JuJu ...there was no reply from her. "I'm sorry I left. I'm sorry I worried you. I didn't find mama. She was gone when I got back but.. I.. I looked for her but.. I. , . I couldn't find her,I couldn't find Mama, Sissy! I've been looking everywhere. Dis city so big and sometimes, sometimes i couldn't eat but,.. and as he began to speak again,

"It's okay", replied Sissy. "Everything is okay now JuJu. Everything is just fine."

JuJu was confused by her response and the look on her face was more of disgust rather than comfort and confusion. What happened to his sister?

Do you like the color red?"Sissy asked as slowly walked by, dragging, looking sluggish and detached from reality. "Do you Juju, do you like red?", she asked him again.

'What is wrong with you Sissy?", JuJu said. Sissy said nothing.

JuJu couldn't take it. He began to yell at her, frustrated and angrily, he grabbed her by the arms and began to shake her.

"SISSY! he repeatedly yelled , 'what's wrong with you?"again and again. Dazed and confused,her eyes lifeless and red, Sissy giggled sadistically. She began to mumble gibberish or what seemed to have been.

"You like it, you think you can get away too..

oh yea... oh yea Bitch... oh yeah mmm hmm ,, ha ha ha , that's what she thought.... you like... say you like it... mm mm that's it..

now crawl bitch.... hahaha..hahahaha... mmmmm hahaaa crraawllll , crawl, crawl"

JuJu stumbled back, falling into the chair, almost down. He felt for the doorknob to the closet door, his safety zone. NO, NO..why did she say those words he asked himself, why? "Crawl"... but mama, … but mama and Red .. no, not Sissy. Sissy was the only pure woman left.

JuJu had no idea that Red paid Sissy a little visit.

JuJu went into the closet and began to hit the walls. He could see the light shining from under the door and he began to have flashes through his mind, but this time, his memory was a little more clear.

In fact, these memories were more vivid, as they were of the man who beat his mother and took her from him, he walked by so cavalier, JuJu felt as if time had just stopped as he paused in that moment to remember.

FLASHBACK

"STUPID BITCH"– (BOOM)...

"Stop... Please. MY BABIES.(")..

"You do what I say you hear me, what I say!"

"Ok.. stop.. please ..ok... ok.. ju .. jus..".

"Just what beg me .. beg Bitch".

.."Please don't make me do this.. please...."

"I want you to get down on your knees and crawl. crawl to me like the fucking little dog you are!

Craw, crawl to your master, Bitch! Now!"

The sound of what would resemble an old slave's beating whip strikes the floor with the force and kicks up dust and fibers from the old carpet. JuJu peeks thru the crack in the door as he sees his mother get sliced across her back with the replica of this tortured piece of history.

Bleeding, as she is crawling to this man, who now sits in awaiting in a chair, with a glass of brown liquor in one hand and a cigarette in the other hand Billy, Red a.k.a continuously yelled and whipped at young Julian's mother. This was the beating he could barely see, but could definitely hear!

These would be the sounds and memories that would torture him. He now had his eyes planted thru the crack but all he saw was Billy. And then he saw her, crawling. She continued to weep and Billy continued to laugh , as the smoke filled the room, he just drank as she bled. JuJu felt numb, helpless and hopeless.
After all, he was only 10.

The cries were almost too much to bear. Blood on the floor, all over her back and the smirk on Billy's face was sickening. Why did mama like him, JuJu asked himself?
He thought to himself, if he could just get the courage to bust out that closet door and do something and save his mother. He couldn't move. Billy's fair, almost white skin intimidated him, not to mention even

sitting in the seat, he was huge.

Billy was a big country boy that came from New Orleans and all anybody knew was he had a little money, a drinking problem, lots of women, a fancy truck and a bad temper. But, women loved him, men feared him but no one, and I mean no one respected him. It has been said that sometimes fear is better to have than respect. In this case, it was true for Billy. He had cheeks like Louis Armstrong when he blew the trumpet, except he stayed that way.

He always had a ragged beard in between a 5 o'clock shadow and actually growing in, sprinkled with gray and red hairs. He was big in stature, like a giant, shadowing the entire floor where JuJu's mother was crawling. His shadow on the wall with the whip intimidated JuJu even more.

His eyes filled with tears, heart ached with guilt , JuJu felt inadequate, weak, insignificant and worthless to everyone , especially his mother. Billy's glass was empty now.

Stepping Off the Stoop

JuJu wasn't so small now, he wasn't stuck, mentally or paralyzed inside that closet anymore, and Billy, he didn't seem so tall anymore either. JuJu was becoming a man before Sissy's eyes. He was changing in every sense of the word. As the months progressed, the years did too. How did these children survive?

JuJu evolved into Julian and Sissy definitely transitioned into Cecilia. But were they still little 14 year old Sissy and 10 year old JuJu when their mother abandoned them?

These two survived a neighborhood infested with drugs prostitution minimal resources ,no support and barely high school educations. Sissy, who liked to be called Cecilia now-although JuJu could not get used to that-was doing her best.

After her first contact with Billy a.k.a. RED , she had never been the same. Honestly, her best was never going to be good enough, especially after what JuJu had seen that she knew nothing about.

His surroundings played a part, but minimal. JuJu's path was chosen for him the moment he hid in that closet. All the hustling Sissy did and love she gave could not erase the images implanted and embedded in his memory. He was traumatized. His issues, his pain and scars cut much deeper than anyone could imagine.

After that day at the store, JuJu was scorned forever. He was abandoned for a second time. When his mother looked him right in his eyes, her own child, and walked away, again, with no hesitation, it changed JuJu! This time, JuJu didn't cry. When he thought he would, but instead he didn't. Juju didn't cry anymore and he no longer even wanted to talk. to his mother ever again.

Sitting on the stoop on one Thursday afternoon, seemed to be a normal day, but would turn out to be the day that would determine what road JuJu would ultimately take.

He was taken back to that night in the closet, the memory he refuses to move on from ...

But would he be stricken with fear or courage?

This would be his test as! Red a.k.a. Billy stops directly in front of him and his shadow covers him completely.

"You just gon' sit there in my way.." He demanded to know.

JuJu was in shock. He couldn't believe he was back, because he had not seen him in years. Why was he back? Sissy appeared in the doorway. JuJu was confused as he stumbled and fumbled over his words, trying to ask Red why he was there, didn't even notice Sissy standing there.

He thought he was imagining things. All JuJu could think to do was run, as Red started to chuckle in the most sinister tone. Before he looked up, JuJu was down by the pond shop which was blocks away.

The days JuJu spent away , he was running numbers for some 'old heads" which a lot of the neighborhood kids did to try to make some money. A few people who dealt with their mom knew JuJu and Sissy's story, so they had somewhat of a soft spot for him. Usually when you start down a particular path with a particular group of people it is not so easy to leave.

A lifestyle in the streets isn't one you just ' decide' to leave . People don't trust those individuals , but in JuJu's case, it was more like charity. They didn't believe he was the snitching or informant type. It made it easier for Juju to come in and make a few dollars here and there, as long as he continued to do right.

JuJu ran a few numbers for a few days, pocketed what he needed and went into that pond shop and walked around until he found exactly what he was looking for. Oddly enough, it was the strangest item he probably ever thought he would purchase. A whip!

What was in his mind and what was he thinking about doing? Did JuJu want to become Red or did he want to use it on him? He never let Sissy see it.

They barely saw each other at all now. After seeing Red a.k.a Billy JuJu disobeyed Sissy every chance he got. Everything was spiraling out of control and Sissy felt hopeless and lifeless.

Save You Save Me

JuJu was in the back practicing his "whipping" as he saw Billy go by and he hadn't seen Sissy all day. So he followed the huge/brutal man closely but not to draw attention. He followed him to a small house that honestly was not what JuJu expected at all

The lawn was freshly manicured, almost to perfection. On the porch sat an oversized rocking chair, a small table, a cane and a newspaper on the ground next to the table. With the curtains drawn, and a squeaky paint chipped screen door, Billy placed the key in the lock and went in.

JuJu didn't know what to do. He was battling himself, his fear, and his need for revenge against Billy, now known as the man Red. This color had become significant to JuJu without him realizing it. The walls, the hands of his sister now realizing *this man was the reason.* He was conflicted and confused, but it did not take long for his fear to be overridden by vengeance. JuJu found an open window from a blowing curtain.

He sat and watched, and as soon as Billy left, JuJu took his chance. He climbed through the window, his heart pounding, his mind racing as to what to do next in the moment. Literally about to fall into the unknown, JuJu could barely hear over his own heartbeat. His pulse felt like it was beating like a drum through his skin.

When he made it inside, he couldn't believe his eyes. The cleanliness of this man was unimaginable to JuJu, someone so evil, brutal, rough, barely even shaven but lived in what JuJu considered to be, compared to his surroundings, elegance and comfort. Everything, literally every little thing was in its place.

JuJu had to be very meticulous in his movements so as to not disturb his surroundings, ensuring to not disturb the perfect environment of Billy's home. JuJu stumbled around what looked like it could be Billy's room.

Slightly different from the remainder of the house, however. JuJu snooped around and eventually came across a small box in a closet.

He sat down and started to sift through things.. old pins, coins, handkerchiefs and... wait no, wait what? HIS MOTHER? Two, three, four, five pictures of her. She and "Red"(a.k.a. Billy) both in pictures, happily without him. JuJu felt numb ,as soon as he saw her face all he could do was stare at the photos.

He starred so long that he fell asleep only to be awakened by voices and footsteps. He readily turned off the light to the closet and not seconds after, Billy entered the room.

JuJu's heart was racing, chest pounding, he was breathing so heavily, he was for certain "Red" could hear. He began to, what sounded like to make a drink, while JuJu sat ,scared out of his mind in the closet.

Now, in the mindset of "Red", he sits in a chair in front of the bed. JuJu hears footsteps approaching closer. Terrified JuJu hid as much as he could not knowing what was about to happen as Red.a.k.a Billy opened the door, but just enough to hang his jacket from the top. Now, JuJu could actually see and hear much clearer.

The sound of JuJu's enemies' voices made him cringe. He intimidated everyone around him but again, *NOT* respected. Suddenly, Red's a.k.a. Billy's tone changed like he was another person. Whoever this woman was JuJu was scared for her.

"Why are you on your feet, you know my rules.... and get to where I can

see you. Get by that window and drop, drop to your knees and crawl"

JuJu's eyes grew larger than life but filled with hate. He despised that word. 'Crawl'.... It was almost a trigger for him .

When he looked through the space in the closet that was cracked, the woman revealed there was no woman at all, it was ... Sissy!

JuJu was paralyzed. He could not believe his eyes. He couldn't understand or comprehend why. He totally and utterly had Sissy's mind hypnotized and had stolen her innocence.

Billy turned "Red" reached from in between the mattress to get his precious possession, the whip. Tears puddled JuJu's eyes and began to fall like a waterfall on his cheeks. Yes, he had purchased the same peculiar item and to inflict the same pain, but to the one who had given it to the one he loved. Now Sissy!! The disbelief was overwhelming but the urge to purge was growing larger.

"I said crawl BITCH",as he slung the whip, hitting Sissy, slashing her legs slightly, but just enough to break skin. Luckily for her, he wasn't as good as he used to be with years of that bottle bringing a few shakes.

Sissy took her beating, she took the ridicule and the shame. The lashing and slashes left and right, as he drank on his whiskey.

He even called her their mothers name a few times proving how demented his mind was.. JuJu cried silently as Sissy cried aloud.

He still felt paralyzed in the closet, stuck like a little boy. Afraid and weak. When she got close to his feet "Red" grabbed the back of Sissy's hair aggressively, looked at her deviously, drunken deeply with the soul and eyes of a demon.

Sissy looked right back at him in those same eyes, pain all over her body, with life lost from her own eyes, pulled a small razor from her bra and quickly as he breathed his whiskey filled breath on her face, slit his throat.

His size and her strength were no longer a factor as he quickly gasped for air grabbing his neck, falling to the floor. JuJu then bursts from the closet and calls Sissy's name. Distraught and in shock, Sissy sits there frozen. JuJu hugs and hugs her but all she could do was sit there on her knees. JuJu just held onto Sissy, as Billy held onto his neck, as he painted the floor RED!

Sissy And Juju